YOU'RE KIDDING, MS WIZ

Terence Blacker has been a full-time writer since 1983. In addition to the best-selling *Ms Wiz* stories, he has written a number of books for children, including *Pride and Penalties* and *Shooting Star* from the *Hotshots* series, *The Great Denture Adventure*, *Nasty Neighbours/Nice Neighbours* and *Homebird*. *Ms Wiz Spells Trouble*, the first book in the *Ms Wiz* series, was shortlisted for the Children's Book Award 1988 and selected for the Children's Book of the Year 1989.

What the reviewers have said about *Ms Wiz*:

'Every time I pick up a Ms Wiz, I'm totally spellbound . . . a wonderfully funny and exciting read.' *Books for Keeps*

'Hilarious and hysterical.' Susan Hill, *Sunday Times*

'Terence Blacker has created a splendid character in the magical Ms Wiz. Enormous fun.' *The Scotsman*

'Sparkling zany humour . . . brilliantly funny.' *Children's Books of the Year*

Titles in the Ms Wiz series

All *Ms Wiz* titles can be ordered at your local bookshop or are available by post from Book Service by Post (tel: 01624 675137).

Terence Blacker

YOU'RE KIDDING, MS WIZ

Illustrated by Tony Ross

**MACMILLAN
CHILDREN'S BOOKS**

This book is dedicated to the children of
The Cedars Primary School, Cranford,
Middlesex

First published 1996 by Macmillan Children's Books

This edition published 1996 by Macmillan Children's Books
a division of Macmillan Publishers Limited
25 Eccleston Place, London SW1W 9NF
and Basingstoke

Associated companies throughout the world

ISBN 0 330 34529 X

7 9 8 6

A CIP catalogue record for this book is available from
the British Library.

Phototypeset by Intype London Limited
Printed by Mackays of Chatham plc, Chatham, Kent

CHAPTER ONE

A Very Regrettable Announcement

All day long, a tall, dark-suited stranger had been seen around the classrooms and corridors of St Barnabas School.

He had wandered in and out of the staff room, a weird, distant smile on his face. At lunch, he had sat in the dining room with the head teacher Mr Gilbert and had picked at his food, nodding seriously as the older man spoke.

He was sitting at the back of Miss Gomaz's classroom as Class Five arrived for their afternoon lesson. When Caroline Smith and Lizzie Thompson smiled at him, he made a note on the pad in front of him. Then Jack Beddows, who had always been something of a big mouth, asked him if he was a school inspector.

For a moment, the stranger had stared back with grey, unblinking eyes. "Not exactly," he said.

"Who *is* that weirdo?" muttered Jack as he sat beside his best friend Podge Harris.

"He's like The Thing From Outer Space," said Podge.

Miss Gomaz walked in. Somehow, she seemed paler than usual and ignored the man in the suit sitting at the back of her classroom.

"We shall be ending today's lesson ten minutes early," she said. "Mr Gilbert has an announcement to make to the whole school."

An announcement? At the end of the school day rather than at Assembly? The children of Class Five looked at one another. It was all very strange.

And it was just about to get even stranger.

*

"Ahem." Mr Gilbert stood before the entire school in the school hall. Although he was a small man, he usually had a sort of bouncy authority to him. But today he looked shrivelled, dusty and old. Standing nearby, the tall, dark-suited stranger seemed to tower over him.

"Ah, well, I expect you're all wondering why I have asked you to gather here today." Mr Gilbert gave a sort of wince. "It's because I have a very important, very regrettable announcement." He hesitated, then took a deep breath. "This morning each of your parents will have received a letter. It tells them—" With a sudden movement, the head teacher reached into his pocket for a handkerchief and blew his nose loudly. When he looked up, his glasses were misted. "It tells them that, at the end of this summer term, St Barnabas School is to close."

There was a gasp from the children in the hall, followed by a confusion of whispered voices.

"But why?" asked Caroline, who was sitting with the rest of Class Five, leaning against the wall to Mr Gilbert's right.

"Why?" The head teacher gave a long and heartfelt sigh. Briefly he seemed to have forgotten what he was going to say, until the tall stranger standing nearby cleared his throat. Mr Gilbert glanced in his direction. "Perhaps I could ask Mr Andrews, the local Education Officer, to explain to you the reasons why St Barnabas has to close."

The Education Officer stepped forward. He clasped his hands in front of him, looked down at the children, then suddenly bared his teeth like a man who has been taking lessons on how to smile but hasn't quite got the hang of it yet. "It is of course a matter of the deepest regret when any educational establishment is forced to close," he intoned.

"Yeah, he looked really upset," muttered Lizzie.

The Education Officer glanced irritably down at Class Five. "Not that I see this as really a closure. It's more an extension of parents' choice to use another school."

"What's he talking about?" said Caroline.

Again the Education Officer paused and stared threateningly at the row of Class Five children before turning back to his audience again. "Which is why a decision has been made, after much heart-searching."

"He'd have to search to find his heart," said Jack.

"So, as from next term" – the Education Officer raised his voice – "the pupils of this school will be absorbed into that of your good friends and neighbours, Brackenhurst Primary School."

"*Brackenhurst*, eurgh!" Podge spoke loudly as if he had just trodden in something disgusting.

"We will, of course, be prepared to listen to your parents' views but I have to say that it would take something very exceptional to make us change our minds."

Podge nudged Jack. "Very exceptional," he whispered. "Maybe this is a case for Ms Wiz."

"Yes!" Several of the children of Class Five picked up Podge's words. The whisper went down the row: "Ms Wiz, it's a case for Ms Wiz, we're going to find Ms Wiz."

The Education Officer had stopped talking and was staring down at Podge.

"Perhaps we could all share this private conversation of yours," he said nastily. "Who or what is wiz?"

"Ah, yes, wiz, er . . . " Podge hesitated, then smiled suddenly. "I was just saying . . . I'm really desperate to go for a wiz," he said.

The Education Officer sighed. "A wiz? What's a . . .? Oh, I see. Yes, all right then."

Winking at Jack, Podge stood up and made his way out of the hall.

Outside, the school was deserted. Podge walked down the corridor and into his classroom. There he sat gloomily at his desk and buried his face in his hands. "Absorbed into Brackenhurst," he moaned. "I don't believe it."

"Bad show, eh?"

Podge looked up. There, sitting on Miss Gomaz's desk, was a rat. It smiled at him. "Yes, old boy, it's me," it said.

Podge had only met one talking, smiling rat in his life. Its name was Herbert and it belonged to Ms Wiz.

"Herbert?" said Podge.

"At your service, old bean," said the rat.

"Good old Ms Wiz." Podge laughed with relief. "She always said she went where magic was needed. We thought she had left the area – we haven't seen her for two years. She must have heard that St Barnabas was in trouble so she sent you along to find out what was—"

"You're joking." Herbert gave a

ratty little laugh. "There is no Ms Wiz these days. She's Mrs Dolores Arnold."

"You mean . . .?"

"Yup. Married," said Herbert. "Married alive. And worst of all—"

At that moment, the sound of children's voices could be heard coming down the corridor.

"Quick," said Podge, grabbing Herbert and putting him inside his jacket pocket.

The door was flung open. "So that's it," said Jack, who was followed by the rest of Class Five. "The best school in the world and they're going to close it down."

"Maybe," said Podge. "And maybe not."

CHAPTER TWO
Dunwizzin

Very few people stared at Podge and Jack as they walked down the High Street after school, which was odd, since Podge was carrying Herbert the rat on his right shoulder.

"I suppose people like to mind their own business," said Jack when Podge pointed this out.

"Either that or they don't want a nipped finger," said Herbert. "I can't stand it when people treat me like some kind of pet. Next street on the left, old bean."

They turned into a narrow, tree-lined street at the end of which, between two larger houses, they saw a tiny cottage almost obscured by roses and ivy. Podge looked at the wooden sign on the garden gate.

"Dunwizzin," he read. "That's a funny name for a house. I wonder what it means."

"When people retire, they call their houses 'Dunroamin'," said Jack. "Ms Wiz must be telling the world that she's retired from magic." He strode up the short garden path and rang the doorbell. "We'll soon see about that," he said.

From inside the cottage came the sound of approaching footsteps. The door was flung open.

"Hi!"

The woman who stood on the doorstep had the long, dark hair of Ms Wiz. She had the slightly surprised look that Ms Wiz used to have. The silver moons which dangled from her ears were exactly the sort of thing which Ms Wiz would once have worn. And yet there was something strangely different about her.

"Er, Ms Wiz?" said Jack nervously.

"Jack!" The woman laughed with pleasure. "Of course it's me." Before Jack could move away, she leant down to kiss his cheek. "Mwa," she said loudly.

Jack stepped back and rubbed his cheek.

"See what I mean?" murmured Herbert to Podge. "She's gone all normal on us."

"Podge!" Ms Wiz was just about to kiss Podge when she saw Herbert on his shoulder. "And there you are, you naughty rat," she said.

"Just don't kiss me, right?" said Herbert.

"Mwa!" Avoiding Herbert, Ms Wiz kissed Podge, then turned back into the cottage. "Come in, come in," she said. "What a gorgeous surprise this is."

"Yeah, gorgeous," said Podge. Glancing at Jack, he followed Ms Wiz into the house.

"I'm afraid it's all a bit of a mess in here," Ms Wiz was saying as she led them through a little hall and into the kitchen. "We've just finished decorating downstairs. D'you like the spring lilac look we've gone for? And what about these adorable fitted units?"

The children stared in amazement.

"Are you feeling all right, Ms Wiz?" asked Podge.

"Yes, of course I am," said Ms Wiz. "Why d'you ask?"

Jack lifted Herbert off Podge's shoulders and put him on the floor. "All this kissing and stuff about gorgeous, adorable, lilac kitchen units – it doesn't seem like you somehow. You've become so . . . homey."

"Ah yes, there's no place like home," smiled Ms Wiz.

"Whatever happened to all the magic?" asked Jack. "You used to be happy going around in a beaten-up old car that used to hover in the air and change into—"

"There's a different kind of magic these days," Ms Wiz said quickly. "The magic of being Mrs Brian Arnold. He'll be home soon."

"So that's all you do these days?" Podge asked. "Hang around your gorgeous, adorable kitchen waiting for your husband to come home? Boy, you've changed."

"Actually," Ms Wiz smiled as she opened a drawer in the kitchen table and took out an exercise book, "I've got a new job."

She handed the book to Podge. "I'm going to be a writer – tell the story of my life. It's going to be a best-seller."

Podge read out the words on the front of the exercise book. *"There's No Business Like Ms Wizness – The Memoirs of a Paranormal Operative."*

"Exciting, eh?" said Ms Wiz.

"Yeah, great," muttered Podge. "So instead of doing magic, you'll be writing about it."

"Exactly," said Ms Wiz. "I know I'm going to *love* writing."

"It's a real shame that you've gone into retirement," said Jack. "We needed a bit of magic after the surprise we were given today."

"Surprise." Ms Wiz held up a finger. "That reminds me. I have a small surprise for you."

She walked out of the kitchen and ran up the stairs.

"She's not listening," said Podge. "She was never exactly good at concentrating but she's all over the place these days."

"Yeah, it's just me, me, me," said Jack.

"And here's my surprise." Ms Wiz stood at the kitchen door. There was

17

a small bundle of white clothes in her arms.

"I don't believe it," said Jack.

"A *baby*?" said Podge.

"Say hello to William," said Ms Wiz. "Otherwise known as the Wiz Kid."

Neither Jack nor Podge had ever had a baby brother or sister in their families. For a few moments, as they looked at William, they behaved in the sort of way they had seen people behaving when a baby was around. They tickled its tummy. They tweaked its tiny toes. They made goo-goo noises.

"Now who wants to hold William?" asked Ms Wiz eventually.

The boys looked at one another.

"Er, no, Ms Wiz," said Podge. "I'm not exactly a baby person, to tell the truth."

"Nor me," said Jack quickly. "I might drop it."

"It? Don't be ridiculous." Ms Wiz gave the baby to Jack. "William's not a thing, you know."

Jack looked down at the tiny figure in his arms as Ms Wiz went to put the kettle on. "Hey, cool baby," he said. William smiled up at him.

"Let's have a go," said Podge, reaching for him.

"Get off," said Jack, holding the baby more tightly. "You can have him in a minute."

"Easy, guys."

Jack and Podge looked at one another, then down at the baby. The tiny voice had seemed to come from the Wiz Kid himself.

"You heard what the lady said — I'm not a thing." William winked deliberately.

"Ms Wiz." Jack frowned. "I think you've got a magic baby here."

"Oh thank you, Jack," said Ms Wiz.

"No, I meant a *magic* magic baby."

"He'll have to be changed soon," said Ms Wiz.

"Changed? Into what?" asked Podge.

Ms Wiz smiled. "His nappies." She took the Wiz Kid and carefully put him in a cot near the window. "Not everything has to be weird and wonderful, you know."

"No," said Podge. "Of course not."

"So you never told me what your surprise was," said Ms Wiz.

"Ah yes, our surprise," said Jack. "Well, yesterday we had a visit from this weirdo hairdo from outer space."

"Weirdo hairdo?"

"He turned out to be an Education Officer." Sitting on the side of the kitchen table, Jack explained everything that had happened that day – how St Barnabas was

21

going to be merged with Brackenhurst.

"*Brackenhurst*?" Ms Wiz looked shocked.

"Exactly," said Jack. "So we badly need your help."

"Hmm." Ms Wiz paced backwards and forwards, deep in thought. "I suppose I could write some letters," she said eventually. "Say what a wonderful school St Barnabas is."

"That's just words, Ms Wiz," said Podge. "We meant something a bit paranormal."

"Paranormal?" Ms Wiz sighed. "I'm not sure about that. When I married Brian, I promised that I wouldn't get involved in magic again."

"But Ms Wiz," Jack pleaded.

Ms Wiz held up both hands. "A promise is a promise," she said.

"There's a parents' meeting at

Podge's house tomorrow," said Jack. "Maybe you could come along as a future parent. What d'you think, Podge?"

Podge seemed to be staring in the direction of the Wiz Kid. A bright white nappy was hovering over the cot and a faint humming sound could be heard from the far side of the kitchen.

"Hm?" Podge returned his attention to the discussion. "Ms Wiz, do your promises apply to William?" he asked.

But Ms Wiz seemed not to be listening. "I'll ask Brian if he can look after William," she said, standing up. "He'll be home soon. I'd better change the Wiz Kid right now."

"I think you might be too late," said Podge.

CHAPTER THREE

No More Magic?

Ms Wiz walked slowly back to the kitchen.

"Normal or paranormal?" she murmured to herself. "Wife or weirdo?"

"Wife *and* weirdo."

Ms Wiz looked down to see Herbert the rat on one of the kitchen chairs.

"Just because you got married, you don't need to change who you are," he said. "To the outside world, you may be Mrs Arnold, but underneath you're still Ms Wiz, paranormal operative."

"Excuse me, Herbert," said Ms Wiz. "I think I can do without a lecture from a rat, thank you very much."

"Think of St Barnabas. All your friends there. Podge, Caroline, Jack, Lizzie, poor shy little Nabila—"

"But you know how Brian hates magic," Ms Wiz sighed. "He thinks it isn't natural to have a wife who can fly and cast spells and talk to her rat."

"*So* old-fashioned," said Herbert. "Oh well, if you're happy to be the little wifey—"

"Enough!" Ms Wiz slapped the

kitchen table with the palm of her hand. "I've told you before that if you don't behave like a normal rat, I'll take you down to the pet shop."

"Normal," grumbled Herbert as he wandered off to the doll's house in the corner where he lived. "Suddenly everything has to be normal."

"Yes, it does." Ms Wiz picked up her exercise book. "Anyway I'm not going to be a little wifey. I'm going to be a best-selling author and let the magic come through in my books."

"Dream on, Dol."

The voice came from the other side of the kitchen where William was leaning over the side of his pram. "Those kids need real magic to save their school, not book magic."

Ms Wiz groaned. "This place is becoming a madhouse," she said. "And I've told you not to call me Dol. If you have to talk to me, at least call me Mummy like other babies do."

"Sure, Dol," said the Wiz Kid.

"I am not going to sit here in my own kitchen being bullied by my baby and my rat," said Ms Wiz firmly. She opened the door into the garden and pushed the pram into the shade of a tree.

"You have an afternoon sleep, while I do some writing."

"You didn't mind me using magic to change my nappies," mumbled the Wiz Kid.

"That's different." Ms Wiz kissed William, then walked back into the kitchen, where she sat at the table. Picking up the exercise book, she turned to the first page and started to read.

Once upon a time I was a paranormal operative. Hardly a day would pass when I didn't do something really rather magical. Sometimes I flew around on a vacuum cleaner. Other

days, I turned teachers into geese or travelled back in time or became Prime Minister for the afternoon. On one occasion, I even used my magic FISH powder to bring characters from books to life.

But that was then and this is now. For the past two years, I have been plain Mrs Dolores Arnold, wife of Brian, mother of William, a happy, ordinary, unmagical person. My family and my lovely home are enough for *me. There's no more need for spells or magic.*

With a weary smile, Ms Wiz laid the exercise book on the table. The trouble was, she thought to herself, she *did* need spells and magic. Spells could be used to keep St Barnabas open. Magic would help bring her book to life. It seemed to her that, however hard she tried, her adventures were never quite as exciting written down as they had been in real life.

"FISH powder," she said to herself thoughtfully. FISH had stood for Freeing Illustrated Storybook Heroes. "I wonder if it would bring my book to life as well." She shook her head. "No, a promise is a promise."

Yet, slowly, as if in a trance, she walked to the kitchen cupboard, murmuring quietly to herself. "On the other hand, maybe a little private magic, just between me and my book, wouldn't make any difference." She took out a small bottle marked "FISH Powder" and carefully sprinkled it over every page of her exercise book.

She had just finished when the door opened.

"Hi, Dolores, I'm home." Brian Arnold stood at the kitchen door. He was tall and dark-haired and wore spectacles which gave him a serious, owlish, tired look.

"Hi, Brian." Ms Wiz kissed her husband.

"Busy day?"

"Quite busy," said Ms Wiz. "Some of my old friends from St Barnabas came round. Apparently there's a plan to close the school."

"Oh dear," said Brian casually. "Where's William?"

"In the garden," said Ms Wiz. "Getting his energy up for staying awake all night."

"Hmm." Casually Brian Arnold picked up Ms Wiz's exercise book and glanced at the pages.

A faint humming noise filled the kitchen. Before Ms Wiz's eyes, a sort of cloud enveloped Brian. When it cleared, an astonishing sight greeted her eyes.

"No more magic, eh?" Herbert laughed quietly from the corner.

"I don't believe it," said Ms Wiz. "So *that's* what the FISH powder does."

CHAPTER FOUR

Such Charming Children

Podge, Lizzie, Jack and Caroline were sitting in a corner in Podge's sitting room, watching as their parents worked on an action plan to save St Barnabas. They had been talking for half an hour. So far there had been no plan and the only action had been when Mr Harris, Podge's father, had spilt his tea while waving his arms about as he made a point.

"All I'm saying is that we've got to work through the right channels," said Mr Harris. "Now it just so happens that I have a few friends in high places on the council. Say the word, I'll pull a few strings – then I'll pass a motion on the education committee."

"Oh Cuthbert," sighed Mrs Harris. "You and your motions."

Mrs Thompson, Lizzie's mother, raised a hand nervously. "Surely we need to get a petition together. Lots and lots of signatures."

"Pop stars," said Jack's father, Mr Beddows, suddenly. "Pop stars are always supporting lost causes."

"How about a party?" suggested Mrs Smith, Caroline's mum. "We could all organize a terrific, huge fund-raising wingding."

"Typical," grumbled Mr Smith,

who was sitting beside her. "Trust my wife to think up another excuse for a party."

"At least I thought of something," snapped Mrs Smith. "The only thing you ever think of is going down to the pub."

"Through the chair, through the chair, *please*." Mr Harris banged the table in front of him. "I call the meeting to order. All those in favour of my passing a motion say Aye."

More voices joined in.

"Who said he was the chairman?"

"What about my party idea?"

"Does anyone know any pop stars?"

The parents were making so much noise that no one except Podge heard the doorbell ring. They were so busy talking that, for several seconds, none of them noticed that someone else had arrived at the meeting and now stood at the door to the sitting room.

"Hullo, who's this?" said Mr Harris at last.

"It's Mrs Arnold," Podge said. "She's come to the meeting as a St Barnabas parent of the future."

"That's no Mrs Arnold," Mrs Thompson laughed. "That's Ms Wiz. I'd recognize her anywhere."

"Wiz? That witch woman?" Mr Harris frowned and folded his arms. "I'll have nothing to do with any paranormal hanky-panky. I'm a respectable man."

"And I'm a respectable woman," said Ms Wiz, smiling. "In fact, I'm a mum – and you can't get much more respectable than that."

"Ms Wiz got married and the magic faded," Jack explained.

"I know the feeling," murmured Mrs Smith, glancing at her husband.

"How old is your baby?" asked Mrs Thompson.

Ms Wiz smiled. "He's almost a year – but he's quite advanced for his age."

"You can say that again," muttered Podge.

"I was wondering whether there was going to be a Beautiful Baby Contest at the school fête?" Ms Wiz asked.

"There always is," said Mrs Thompson. "But what's that got to do with saving St Barnabas?"

"I think I'll enter William," said Ms Wiz firmly. "And will there be a book stall?"

"I'm looking after that," said Mrs Beddows. "Any old volumes are welcome."

"What about a new volume?" asked Ms Wiz. She reached into the bag hanging over her shoulder and took out her purple exercise book.

As she opened the book, Jack nudged Podge. "She's wearing black nail varnish," he whispered. "You know what that means."

Ms Wiz held the book open in front of the parents. "I was wondering if there would be a market for my memoirs," she said.

"Black nail varnish," said Podge quietly. "Maybe the magic hasn't faded."

As if in reply, a strange humming noise could be heard and a thick mist filled the room.

"Books and babies," Mr Harris was muttering. "I've never heard anything so . . . *I want my mummy!*"

As the mist cleared, an extra-ordinary sight was revealed. In the place of the seven parents stood seven children. Amongst them, a small, fat boy was crying. The rest were looking around, confused.

"Eh?" Jack stared in amazement. "What's going on?"

"Just an experiment, Jack." Ms Wiz smiled. "I told you my writing was magical."

"But who are these people?" asked Podge.

"They're your parents," said Ms Wiz. "When I put some magic powder on the pages, my book seems to take its readers back to their childhood."

"I want my mummy!" Mr Harris's small, round face had turned the colour of a tomato.

"He's rather sweet, your dad," Jack
said to Podge.

Podge shook his head in disbelief.
"He's even fatter than I am," he said.
"And he always told me he was thin
when he was a child."

"He certainly seems to have
forgotten about his motion," said Ms
Wiz.

"Look at my parents," whispered
Caroline. "They're holding hands.
I've never seen them do that before."

Mr Harris had turned to Podge. "Have *you* seen my mummy?" he sniffed miserably.

"Granny? I mean, your mum? Er, not since last Christmas, no," said Podge.

Tears welled up once more in Mr Harris's eyes.

"Ms Wiz, this is getting too weird for me," said Podge. "I can't get used to being four years older than my father."

"Jolly interesting." Ms Wiz sat on a chair nearby to watch.

"Such charming children." She sighed. "And then they grew up."

"But these aren't really children," said Caroline with a hint of panic in her voice. "Could we have our parents back now, please?"

"Honestly," sighed Ms Wiz. "First you want magic, then you don't." She took the bottle of FISH powder from her pocket, stood up and

41

sprinkled it over the seven children. "REDWOP HSIF! REDWOP HSIF!" she muttered.

As the loud humming noise returned, the room was once again obscured by a heavy mist.

" . . . it's all a load of nonsense is what I say." Podge's dad, as large and as adult as he had ever been, stood among the parents.

Mr and Mrs Smith were staring at one another in amazement. They were still holding hands. Slowly they both smiled.

"I mean, a bloomin' book's not going to change anything, is it?" said Mr Harris, turning to the four children. "What are you lot staring at?" he asked.

"He was such a shy little boy, your dad," said Jack. "I wonder what changed him."

"I'll tell you this, my lad. When I was a young 'un, I kept my mouth shut and minded my own business," said Mr Harris.

"Yeah, Dad," said Podge. "Of course you did."

Ms Wiz picked up her exercise book and slipped it back into her shoulder bag. "A very successful experiment, I think," she said quietly. "Now for the school fête."

CHAPTER FIVE

Shazam

Apart from the big banner reading "SOS! SAVE OUR SCHOOL", which had been draped over the wire surrounding the playground, the St Barnabas School fête was much like any other.

On a platform that had been erected in front of the school, Mr Gilbert was making announcements into a microphone. The Lady Mayoress, who had opened the fête, stood nearby, looking large and regal. In the background, the iron-grey head of the Education Officer could be seen bobbing about with nervous self-importance.

"Where *is* she?" said Jack, who was standing with Podge beside Mrs Thompson's cake stall.

"Mm?" Podge took a bite of the bun in his hand and began chewing slowly.

"Ms Wiz promised to be here," said Jack, scanning the playground with his eyes.

Podge swallowed. "Probably that husband of hers," he said. "It didn't sound as if he was too happy about Ms Wiz coming out of retirement." He took another bite of the bun.

Looking at him, Jack shook his head. "Gross," he muttered.

"It'sh shtreshh," protested Podge, spraying Jack with crumbs. "When I'm stressed, I have to eat," he said. "And I get particularly stressed if one of Mrs Thompson's buns is near me."

"Make way, make way!" At that moment, there was a commotion from the gates to the playground. Wearing a bright orange trouser suit, Ms Wiz could be seen carving her

way through the crowd, a pram in front of her.

"Over here, Ms Wiz," shouted Jack.

"Phew, I knew we should have flown. The traffic was terrible." Ms Wiz pushed her hair out of her eyes. "Brian's coming along later."

Podge looked into the pram. "All right, Will?" he said.

The Wiz Kid lifted his tiny thumb and winked.

"Last call for the Beautiful Baby

Contest," Mr Gilbert was saying.

"All right." Ms Wiz looked around her and dropped her voice. "Here's the plan." She reached under the blanket in the pram, took out her purple exercise book and handed it to Jack. "You give my book to the Education Officer. He reads it and – shazam!"

"Shazam?" said Jack.

"He'll be putty in your hands once he's a child," Ms Wiz smiled. "Children always do what they're told."

"I can tell you haven't been a mum for long," said Podge.

"But where will you be?" asked Jack.

"We'll be winning the Beautiful Baby Contest."

"Yeah!" A tiny voice could be heard from the pram. "Going for gold!"

"Oh, and you'll need this." Ms Wiz

reached into her pocket and took out a small bottle. "When you want to undo the spell, just sprinkle some powder over the Education Officer and say "FISH POWDER" backwards – that's 'HSIF REDWOP'."

"HSIF REDWOP," said Jack carefully trying to remember the spell.

"But this is crazy, Ms Wiz," said Podge desperately. "You're meant to be the Paranormal Operative round here, not us."

Ms Wiz shrugged helplessly. "A promise is a promise," she said, turning the pram towards where the other mothers and babies were gathering.

"Thanks for nothing, Ms Wiz," Podge muttered as they watched her walk away. "So how are we going to get the Education Officer to change his mind?"

Jack was tapping the tip of his nose, a sure sign that a cunning idea

was occurring to him. "A promise is a promise," he said quietly. "OK, Podge. Here's what we do ... "

Moments later, they were walking over to the platform where the Education Officer was seated next to Mr Gilbert.

"Peter, Jack." The head teacher smiled down at them. "How are you enjoying the fête?"

"Very much," said Jack. "We have a present for the Education Officer."

"A present?" The Education Officer turned slowly to them.

"Class Five wanted to apologize for interrupting your announcement last week," said Podge in his most angelic voice.

The Education Officer turned to Mr Gilbert. "Maybe you were right about this class of yours," he murmured. "Sometimes they seem almost human."

Mr Gilbert narrowed his eyes suspiciously. "I'll believe it when I see it," he said.

"So where is this present of mine?" asked the Education Officer.

"In the classroom, sir," said Jack with an innocent smile. "Would you like us to take you there?"

Looking slightly embarrassed, the Education Officer followed Jack and Podge into the school building, along the corridor and into Class Five's classroom. While Podge closed the door behind them, Jack slipped the purple exercise book on to one of the desks.

"Ah, here it is, sir," he said, picking it up again and handing it to the Education Officer.

"This is our class project," said Podge. "It's all about things that happened to us when we were in Class Three. We called it *There's No Business Like Ms Wizness*."

"What a funny title."

"That's explained inside, sir," said Jack. "Maybe you'd like to read it."

The Education Officer opened the purple exercise book and stared at the first page. Within seconds, the classroom was filled with the sound of a humming noise and a thick, choking mist.

When the mist cleared, the Education Officer was nowhere to be seen. In his place stood a small boy with neatly parted hair.

"Hello," he said, with a shy smile. "My name is Laurence Andrews. My friends call me Larry."

"Hi, Larry," said Jack.

"Have we met?" asked the little boy.

"Er, not exactly," said Podge.

Jack sat down at one of the desks and let out a long, heartfelt sigh. "We have got *such* a problem, Larry," he said miserably. "A horrid man has just told us that our school is going to be closed down."

"Oh dear," said Larry.

Podge slumped down tragically at the next-door desk. "We're all going to be sent away to another school, full of lots of big boys and girls who are real bullies," he sniffed.

"Oh dear oh dear," said Larry, the corners of his mouth turning down, his chin trembling.

"Our teachers will all be fired and the buildings torn down," said Jack quietly. "All gone . . . our games, our friendships, our special football team." He stared out of the window. "And we were all *so* happy here too."

Tears had filled Larry's eyes. "Stop it, stop it, I can't stand it," he sobbed. "If only there were something I could do."

Podge shook his head. "The only thing you can do is promise that, when you grow up, you'll never have anything to do with closing down a nice school like this one."

"Close a school down?" Larry looked shocked. "Why on earth would I want to do that?"

"Just promise, please," said Jack.

"All right, all right, I promise," said Larry. "That's the one thing I'll never ever do."

"Thanks, Larry." Jack stood up, the bottle of FISH powder in his hand.

He sprinkled some on the little boy's neat hair. "FISH FLIP FLOP," he said.

Nothing happened.

"Er, HASIF REDMOP?" tried Jack.

"Excuse me, but what are you doing?" asked Larry.

"It's HSIF REDWOP," said Podge, "HSIF—" And, before he had finished, the classroom was once again filled with a dense mist.

As it cleared, the Education Officer stood where Larry had been seconds before. "Now where were we?" He wiped his eyes and found to his surprise that the back of his hand appeared to be damp with tears.

"We were explaining what a special school St Barnabas is," said Jack. "All our friends . . . We are all so happy here."

The Education Officer frowned as if some distant memory was coming back to him.

"And that you seem to us the
sort of person who would never
have anything to do with closing
down a nice school like this one,"
said Podge. "That was the
one thing you would never ever
do."

The Education Officer blinked and
looked around him as if seeing the
classroom for the first time. Then he
stared out into the playground,
thronging with happy children,

parents and teachers. "I once made a promise," he whispered.

"A promise is . . . a promise," said Jack.

"You're right." Tucking Ms Wiz's purple exercise book under his arm, the Education Officer walked slowly to the door. "A promise *is* a promise. Maybe it's not too late."

"Go for it, Larry," smiled Jack.

The Education Officer hesitated at the door. "Larry? No one's called me that since I was at school."

"Cool name," said Podge.

"Thank you." The Education Officer left the room, shaking his head as if something very odd had happened to him.

Through the window, Jack and Podge watched as the Education Officer walked to the platform and picked up the microphone. "I have an announcement to make," he said. "It's about St Barnabas School . . . "

Seconds later, a great cheer echoed around the playground.

Sprinting across the playground, Jack and Podge found Ms Wiz and the Wiz Kid near the entrance.

"We did it!" shouted Podge.

"It worked!" Jack laughed, waving the bottle of FISH powder.

"Welcome to the world of magic." Ms Wiz smiled as she took the bottle and put it in her bag.

"Huh, *now* she likes magic," William muttered loudly from the pram.

"What happened in the Beautiful Baby contest?" asked Podge.

Ms Wiz sighed. "The Lady Mayoress looked into the pram and said, 'What a chubby little chap he is.' So William decided to reply."

"I only told her she was no bloomin' supermodel herself,"

grumbled William. "What was wrong
with that?"

"Hi, Dolores." From behind them,
Brian Arnold, Ms Wiz's husband,
appeared. "Sorry I'm late. Did I miss
anything?"

"You could say," said Jack.

"Not much," said Ms Wiz.

They were interrupted by Mrs
Hicks making an announcement
from the platform. "We have a lost
child," she said, looking down at a

small six-year-old in shorts who was standing beside her. "He says his name is Henry Gilbert."

"Sounds like you've got another reader," said Podge quietly. "That magical book of yours has just taken the head teacher back to his childhood."

"Magical book?" Mr Brian Arnold narrowed his eyes. "Have you been up to your tricks again?"

"Tricks? Not me." Ms Wiz reached into her bag and took out a small bottle of powder. She kissed her husband lightly on the cheek, then winked at Jack and Podge. "A writer's work is never done," she said.